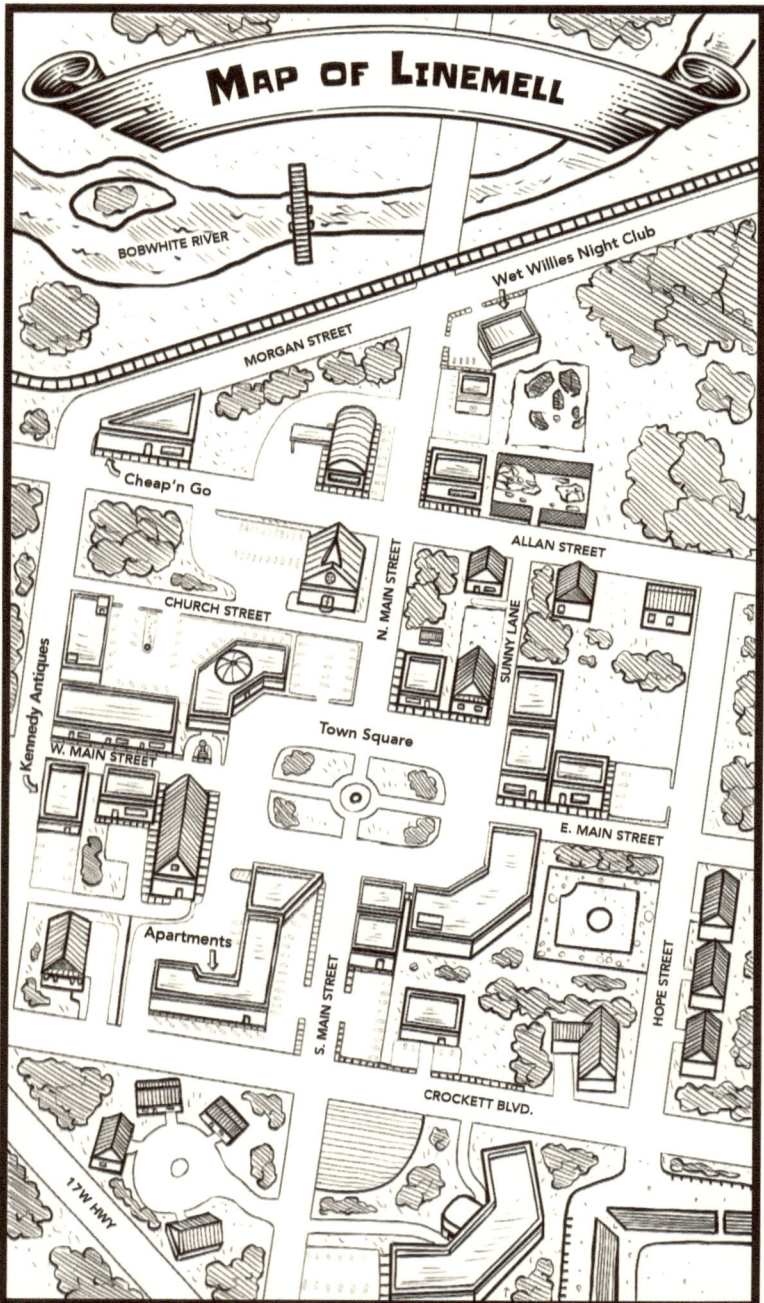

THE CURIOUS WORLD OF · EDDIE BILLINGS ·

BOOK 1

EDDIE
& THE LIZARD MAN

by
Stefan Liner
Robin Liner

Illustrated by Josef Liner

LINER HOUSE

An imprint of
EAST STREAM GROUP, LLC
Weaverville, NC

Liner House is an imprint of East Stream Group, LLC
Weaverville, NC 28787

EDDIE & THE LIZARD MAN
Copyright © 2020 by East Stream Group, LLC

This book is a work of fiction. Names, characters, business-es, organizations, places, events and incidents either are the product of the author's imagination or are used ficti-tiously. Any resemblance to actual persons, living or dead, events, or locales is entirely coincidental.

Library of Congress Cataloging-in-Publication Data
Library of Congress Control Number: 2020914303

ISBN 13: 978-0-9910342-4-6 (Paperback)
ISBN 13: 978-0-9910342-7-7 (Hardback)
ISBN 13: 978-0-9910342-5-3 (eBook)

Book and Cover design by East Stream Studio
Illustrations by Josef Liner

For information on all Liner House publications
visit our website at www.linerhouse.com

First Edition: August 2020

1 2 3 4 5 6 7 8 9 10

Printed in the United States of America

TABLE OF CONTENTS

1

A Particularly
Interesting Find

In the center of the small town of Linemell, a place shrouded with its own curious secrets, crept a quaint road named Main Street. On one side of the street were family-owned shops and restaurants, and on the other side stood a towering, old brick building that dated back to the time of the great pioneer, Daniel Boone. In fact, one of the town's proudest moments was the night Daniel Boone slept in Minnie Ponder's spare bedroom in that very building.

However, since then the building had changed hands a number of times. Mrs. Ponder eventually sold the building to a businessman who turned it into a hardware store. Then, that businessman's grandchildren, who inherited the building, sold it to another businessman that turned it into a mattress store. After a good run, that businessman retired, closed the store and the space remained vacant for a number of years. That is, until another businessman, Kevin Kennedy, moved into the area and opened an antique shop in the tired, old building; an antique shop called Kennedy Antiques.

Now, if you've never been in one, there is something wonderfully mysterious about an antique shop. They are filled with fascinating items like old dressers with secret compartments and shelves stacked with leather-bound books and clocks and vases.

It's the perfect kind of place for a bird lover to find an 1879 carving of a cardinal. Or the perfect kind of place for a cartographer to find a hand drawn map of the Pigeon River. But even more than that, it was the perfect kind of place for someone like Eddie Billings to take a part-time job, or at least that is what he thought when he took the job.

But who is Eddie Billings? Well, one could say Eddie was an awkward sort of guy of average height with light brown hair and inquisitive blue eyes. That he usually dressed in mismatched clothes found at a thrift store or that he didn't have many friends or get out enough. And all of those things might be true.

However, the most important things to know about Eddie Billings are that he was an overly-curious conspiracy theorist, junk food enthusiast, tinkerer and, in this particular moment, a disinterested antique store clerk, who was dusting off a porcelain angel figurine when his eye caught a clock sitting on top of an old bookcase - it read 2:50 p.m. He thought to himself...

"Only ten more minutes. Only ten more minutes and my shift is over. If I'm lucky, maybe today's shift will be a good one."

Now, Eddie's shift began at 1:00 p.m. and ended at 3:00 p.m. Monday through

Friday. His main responsibilities were to assist customers, arrange inventory, and keep the place clean, which was what he was occupied with at the moment... Well, that - and counting down the minutes to 3:00 p.m.

You see, Eddie didn't mind arranging inventory or keeping things clean. He could do that all day long and be quite content. It was assisting customers that made Eddie anxious. That's why a "good shift" to Eddie was a shift that *didn't* involve assisting customers or even seeing a customer. So far, today's shift had been a good one.

So with only ten minutes left on the clock, Eddie remained pessimistically optimistic that this shift could actually end up being one of the rare and cherished "good ones."

As Eddie continued cleaning various items arranged on various counter-tops, shelves, and display cases, he heard a faint, dissonant whirring sound coming from the back of the dimly-lit antique store. Intrigued, he slowly peeked his head around the corner of a large wooden dresser. He looked toward the dark hall that led to the back office where his boss, Kevin, worked behind closed doors.

As Eddie peered down the ominous hall, suspicion surrounding the strange noise began to fill his mind.

"What is that, a fan? No, it can't be. The pitch changes too much. A radio? No, there's not any static. Maybe it's some sort of communication device..."

Then Eddie had an epiphany...

"Like an alien communication device!"

Now, granted, an alien communication device isn't the kind of thing to jump into most people's minds. But then Eddie isn't like most people. Remember, he's an overly-curious conspiracy theorist. And overly-curious conspiracy theorists are very good at coming up with creative explanations for things that seem out of place.

So, with the misplaced noise ringing in his ears, Eddie resumed his dusting and speculating.

"Could that actually be an alien communication device? If so, why is it in Kevin's office?"

Looking for the next item to clean, Eddie

saw a remarkably filthy old milk bottle sitting on the lower shelf of a bookcase. He crouched down to grab it. As he did, he thought to himself,

"I just don't get it. An old milk bottle being sold for eighteen bucks. Who in their right mind buys an old..."

Eddie's thoughts were interrupted when he saw something very peculiar, yet lately, increasingly more familiar.

"Another one!" He said under his breath.

There, lying behind the milk bottle, was a snake-like shedding of skin.

The reason Eddie said "another one," was because in the past week alone he'd found ten such skins. But the truly interesting part was that in the four years he'd worked at the store he'd never once seen a snake. This caused Eddie to wonder whether they actually belonged to snakes at all.

"Whoa, that's a big one!"

Eddie held it up for inspection, then proceeded to carefully place it in his shirt pocket. From the same pocket he removed a notepad and pen, items that never left his person. On the cover of the notebook were the words…

MY PARTICULARLY INTERESTING FINDINGS

Looking down at his wristwatch he read the time, 2:53 p.m. He found a blank page in his notepad and jotted down the time, date, and location where he found the skin. He also added a note about the strange whirring noise coming from the back office.

As he was writing, a loud bell rang out, startling him. It was the front doorbell, and to Eddie's dismay, someone had arrived.

2

THE NAIL & THE
COFFIN

Eddie was hunched over out of sight
when someone's voice filled the room.
"Hello? Is anybody here?"

This word was not your typical hello. It
had been turned into three syllables that
were more sung than spoken, hel-lo-oh.

That *someone* was a middle-aged woman
named Susan, who strolled into the shop with
her heels clicking confidently toward the front
counter. She wore overpowering lilac perfume
and carried a gold snake-skin handbag.

Susan sold antiques Online and often

brought items into the store for Eddie's boss, Kevin, to appraise. She was a serious individual and due to her stern countenance Eddie found himself intimidated by her. Understandably, the ensuing interaction was one Eddie had hoped to avoid entirely, and he would have done so, had Susan arrived a mere eight minutes later.

Unfortunately, that's not what happened and any chance of this shift ending as a good one had been lost. So, letting out a sigh of defeat, Eddie put the pen and pad back into his pocket with his newly-found, particularly interesting snake-skin, and hesitantly revealed himself from behind the bookcase.

"Back here."

"Oh, hi, Eddie," she called from across the room, her voice dripping with disappointment, "Where's Kevin?"

"He's in the back," Eddie replied flatly.

Eddie fumbled through a cluster of tables that seemed to be purposefully trying to hinder him from reaching the service counter. Susan, on the other hand, moved quite unhindered toward the same destination. Each step from her emerald-green high heels sounded like a hammer striking a nail into the coffin representing her low estimation of Eddie. At least that's the way her footsteps sounded to him.

As he rounded the last table, a flustered Eddie accidentally bumped a lamp sitting near the table's edge. The lamp toppled. Thankfully, Eddie had quick reflexes and caught the fragile merchandise before any damage was done. But by the time he had returned the lamp back to its place, Susan had taken her final steps and arrived at the counter.

On hearing the last step of her heels hit the stained vinyl floor, Eddie felt that his fumbling had resulted in yet another rusty nail being set in that proverbial coffin of the woman's low appraisal of him. He wondered how many more nails were going to be set before Susan decided the lid had been sufficiently sealed.

Letting out a sigh of resignation, Eddie plastered onto his face a very, very, very superficial smile. The kind of smile that says, "I'm smiling on the outside, but frowning on the inside." Yes, it was with that kind of smile that Eddie finished the journey from the bookcase to the counter where Susan was impatiently awaiting his arrival.

3

FIVE MEASLY MINUTES

Eddie could tell that Susan was frustrated with the fact that she had to interact with *him* instead of Kevin. So, in an effort to lighten the mood, Eddie tried pointing out something positive.

"But at least Kevin finished the appraisal for you... so that's a good thing."

The appraisal Eddie was referring to was for an extraordinarily worthless vase that sat on the counter in front of Susan. Kevin had called Susan earlier that day to let her know the vase was ready to be picked up and was worth much less than she paid for it. Eddie assumed this was the reason for her extra-sour mood. I say *extra*-sour mood because as far as Eddie was concerned Susan was usually in a *moderately* sour mood. And who could blame her? The woman wasn't very good at buying antiques. Which was surprising because she seemingly did it for a living. But that's beside the point. The point is Susan was in an extra-sour mood and Eddie was on the receiving end.

"Right," Susan snorted. "I can see that the vase is ready, Eddie. But where is the appraisal *document*?"

"Huh?"

"The appraisal *document*. The piece of paper that shows how much the vase is worth?"

Eddie looked down at the counter. She was right. The document wasn't there. So, he frantically, but not too frantically, began scanning and shuffling through a myriad of other papers scattered across the counter in hopes of finding the appraisal document. But no matter how hard he looked it just wasn't there.

He prayed as he searched,

"Please be here, please be here. Come on, show yourself."

As Eddie continued in vain to find what wasn't there, Susan began to rattle off reason after reason why the appraisal document was so important and why she couldn't leave without it. Eddie glanced down at his wristwatch, it read 2:54 p.m. He still had six minutes before Kevin would be finished with his office work and Kevin was adamant about not being disturbed before that time. As a matter of fact, not being disturbed during his sacred "office work" was Kevin's only non-negotiable rule. A rule Eddie had no intention of breaking. So, he knew he had to figure something out fast.

Just then, an idea popped into his mind. An idea that might make the whole horrible situation go away. So, Eddie stood upright and decided to give it a try.

"Um, it seems as if Kevin may still have the document back in the office. But this isn't a problem because I can just have him email it to you. What's your email address?"

Eddie found a piece of scratch paper

and pulled the pen out of his pocket. He prepared to write down her email but instead of being agreeable, Susan said...

"No. That won't work. I need the original... were you not listening to a word I just said?"

Eddie glanced up at a wall clock just over Susan's shoulder. It read 2:55 p.m. He still had five minutes left and the email idea was a complete failure. This failure was compounded by the fact that Susan had a profound hatred of waiting for anything, a fact that Eddie and everyone in Linemell were well aware of. Nevertheless, that's what Eddie had to do, convince her to wait. He could only hope she would understand.

"Well, I would go get the original, but the thing is, Kevin's not supposed to be disturbed for another five minutes... So, I don't know, maybe you could just look around..."

Before Eddie could finish his proposition, a very irritated Susan quite figuratively jumped down the poor man's throat.

"Five minutes!? Five measly minutes!" Susan rambled on angrily.

Okay, pause. Now, Eddie was in a predicament because despite his hopes, Susan in her predictably impatient fashion, didn't see *why* interrupting Kevin five minutes before 3:00 p.m. was such a big deal. But Eddie knew that the consequences of disturbing Kevin five minutes *or even ten seconds* before 3:00 p.m. were exponentially greater than the discomfort of aggravating Susan at that moment.

So, you see the problem? They both saw five minutes in completely different ways, and anytime two people see the same thing differently, it usually means that something interesting is about to happen. And something interesting was about to happen. Okay, back to our story.

"Five minutes? You know what, why don't I just go get it myself. He's right back there, isn't he?"

Without another word, Susan maneuvered around the counter and made her way toward the hallway that led to Kevin's office. Eddie's eyes filled with terror as he contemplated Kevin's reaction to being interrupted five minutes before 3:00 p.m.

4

A Courageous Moment

Eddie knew that if he wanted to keep his job, he had to keep Susan from storming in on Kevin. So, he ran around the counter and back through the tables, calling after Susan to stop. But she had no intention of stopping.

Then somehow, from somewhere deep within, Eddie did one of the bravest things he's ever done. He jumped through a narrow gap between two fairly valuable tables and cut Susan off. He stood there between her and the hallway like a heavy castle gate.

19

Then from an even deeper place than the last, Eddie felt his back straighten, his chest puff out, and his chin grow stern.

"I'll go!" Eddie said bravely.

Susan was taken by surprise. So was Eddie. But for some reason his mouth kept saying words. He expressed those words with bolstered courage.

"I'll go!" He continued with bravado, and used as many words as he could think of so as to use up as much time as possible, "I will go back there to Kevin's office and I will get the appraisal document."

Susan was about to speak, but Eddie pressed on.

"...And once I have it in my hand, I will bring it back out here to you. Then, I will place the document into your hand and you, you will have it… in your hand."

Eddie paused to think of more things he could say in order to kill the time. Susan, however, somewhat mesmerized by Eddie's declaration, but at the same time still feeling very impatient, took hold of the opportunity and responded in frustration…

"Okay!" Then, gesturing toward Kevin's office with her fingers, she added, "Just go."

Eddie spoke with relief, "Great! I'll go right now."

"Great," Susan replied wearily.

Eddie hesitantly backed toward the dark hallway, telling himself this would all work out. That he would get the appraisal document for Susan and wouldn't get fired or yelled at by Kevin. After all, now it was only four minutes until 3:00 p.m. and most people know that four minutes is entirely different from five. He just hoped that Kevin saw four minutes the same way.

As Eddie slowly inched closer and closer to the entrance of the hall he addressed Susan with a forced confidence.

"Should only take a sec."

After a couple more steps he looked down at his watch and added under his breath,

"Four minutes at the most."

With just one more step Eddie had arrived. He could feel warm stale air coming out of the darkness, pressing down on his shoulders. An odd stench filled his nostrils, causing him to hold his breath. He looked up at Susan one last time, hoping that somehow she could appreciate the weight of this moment and the immense risk he was putting himself in.

But that was not to be. For there she stood with arms crossed, waiting for him to take the step. No, Eddie was alone. No one was rooting for him. No one cared what might lay ahead of him at the end of the hall. Yet, he must press on.

He gave Susan one last unconvincing smile. The kind of smile grown-ups give each other when there is something they don't want to do, but know they have to do it anyway. Yes, that is the kind of smile Eddie had on his face as he turned to enter the very long dark hallway. But even that smile slowly melted away as he took his first step into the darkness.

5

THE VERY LONG DARK HALLWAY

For many people it is not what they can see that scares them most. Rather, it is what they can't see. The unknown. It's the thought of what could be lurking in the shadows or just around the corner that really frightens them. And this is what made Eddie so uneasy every time he had to venture down the dark twisting corridor that led to Kevin's office. The lighting was poor, and the path was obstructed by furniture and other items stacked along the wall or hanging from the ceiling.

23

Another reason for Eddie's apprehension about interrupting Kevin was because he never knew which Kevin he was going to get. On one hand Kevin could be quite congenial and even charming. However, on the other hand, he could be very snappy, domineering, and scary. To Eddie, there was something very, very different about the two versions of Kevin, something very different indeed. He was like Dr. Jekyll and Mr. Hyde. Nonetheless, Eddie gathered himself together and bravely maneuvered down the corridor toward Kevin's office.

As Eddie prepared himself for the myriad of ways Kevin might react to being interrupted before 3:00 p.m., the strange whirring noise he heard earlier that day slowly meandered down the hall to Eddie's inquisitive ears. Looking ahead, he could see a faint reddish light shining through a crack between the door and door frame of Kevin's office. Eddie found that strange. Kevin usually kept the door closed.

Eddie came to an abrupt stop about six feet away from the door and looked down. There on the floor was a worn piece of duct tape with the words "Do Not Pass" written on it. Another rule Eddie had no intention of breaking.

So, instead of reaching across the line to knock on the door, Eddie decided to courteously call out to Kevin from the side of the line of which he presently stood. But just as he opened his mouth to speak, Eddie noticed the strange whirring noise stopped, and was replaced by an eerie silence. An eerie silence soon broken by an equally eerie sound, the sound of Kevin's voice. Eddie noticed it sounded slightly different than usual.

Slowly looking up from the warning tape, Eddie leaned forward ever so slightly to get a better view into the office. Kevin's back was to Eddie as he sat at a large black desk with a phone to his ear.

"Hello, It'sss Kevin. I got the messs- age about tonight. Yessss, sssseven will be fine."

Kevin's voice was low and hard to hear so Eddie leaned in a little closer, being sure not to cross the "Do Not Pass" line.

"Of courssse I'm nervoussss, but I'm convinsssed now more than ever that it'sss time to sssstop exsssperimenting and do it for real. No, tonight'sss the night. It'sss gotta be tonight. Okay, sssee you sssoon. Bye."

Eddie's mind was filled with suspicion as he contemplated everything he just seen and heard. And although many questions were bouncing around his head, the one question that echoed louder than all the others was...

"What does Kevin mean by 'it's time to stop experimenting and do it for real?'"

Then quite abruptly, another thought bombarded his mind,

"Oh, no. Susan! She's still waiting."

6

"Do Not Pass"

Eddie looked back over his shoulder toward the front of the shop where he knew Susan was waiting for the appraisal document. Then he looked down at his watch. It read 2:58 p.m.

Wincing, he turned to call Kevin, but his voice went mute when he saw Kevin already standing in front of him. Directly in front of him. Quite literally 6 inches in front of him.

Startled, Eddie thought to himself...

"How did he get out here so fast... and without making a sound?"

Eddie tried finding Kevin's eyes in the darkness but Kevin's face remained in shadow. All that was visible was his mouth. The mouth opened and Eddie felt a blast of Kevin's stale breath cross his face as Kevin screeched,

"Have you forgotten that there are consssequensssesss for breaking the rulesss?!"

Terrified, Eddie responded with as much poise as he could muster,

"No sir, it's just..." He fumbled with his words, "I mean, I know it's not technically 3:00 p.m. yet, but Susan..."

Kevin interrupted Eddie. The volume in Kevin's voice increased and the pitch rose as he hissed on,

"Two hoursss, Eddie. You work for two hoursss a day. 1 p.m. to 3 p.m. During which, I am Not. To. Be. Disssturbed."

"I know that, and I'm sorry. It's just that Susan needs the appraisal document for the vase."

Kevin's nasally voice rang out, "The appraisssal document for the vassse!"

At that moment Eddie thought for sure he was about to lose his job. Traditionally, whenever Kevin would repeat something someone else said, it meant Kevin was very vexed by the person who had just spoken.

Suddenly, something strange happened. Almost in the blink of an eye, the whole atmosphere completely changed. Granted, it was still dark, but the place somehow lost that stale smell. Kevin stepped backwards a little, allowing a soft light to cross his face that revealed his bright green eyes. An odd charm suddenly came over him.

"Of course. I must have forgotten to set it out there. Let me get it."

And, just like that, again in the blink of an eye, Kevin was speaking normally. He walked back into his office and emerged seconds later with the appraisal document in his hand. He closed the office door behind him and leisurely stepped past Eddie as he made his way down the hall. To Eddie's surprise, Kevin came to a deliberate stop about halfway down the corridor. And without turning, Kevin addressed Eddie in a smooth steady voice,

"Eddie?"

"Uh, yes sir?"

"What time did Susan arrive?"

Eddie thought for a second then answered, "A few minutes before 3:00 p.m."

There was a brief silence, followed by one word from Kevin's unseen mouth, "Interesting."

With that one word Kevin let out a long sigh and exited the very long dark hallway.

As Eddie stood alone in the darkness, he looked down at his wristwatch. The time read 3:01 p.m.

Perplexed by what he had witnessed in the past ten minutes, a theory began to form in Eddie's head. A theory that followed him all the way home.

7
A FRIEND, NOT A PET

Back at Eddie's apartment... sorry, apartment is too generous a term. Let's use the term... living quarters. You see, Eddie's living quarters couldn't really be referred to as an apartment because technically it wasn't one. It was actually a utility room where the owner of the building allowed Eddie to live in exchange for maintenance services.

So, allow me to start again. Back at his living quarters, which was a small single room space about six feet wide by eight feet long, Eddie took a glass jar from the top of one of his many shelves and placed into it the snake-like skin he found earlier that day. The jar was labeled...

REPTILIAN SHEDDINGS

...and was filled with skins similar to the one Eddie just added. He did this while recounting some of the things he overheard Kevin saying in his office.

"...and then Kevin said, 'tonight is the night,' but in a very suspicious way."

Now, you may be wondering who Eddie was telling this to. Well, Eddie was talking to Dog, a smallish beagle that was more a friend than a pet. And actually, he was very much more a friend than a pet because Eddie didn't technically own Dog. He did feed Dog on a fairly frequent basis, but many friends have similar relationships where one friend does the majority of the eating and the other does the majority of the feeding.

In fact, the only reason Dog was permitted to be on the premises was because he was a friend and not a pet. You see, the landlord of the building had a "No Pets" rule, so it was important that Dog remained solely a friend.

As a friend, Dog was often a sounding board for Eddie's thoughts, ideas, and theories. He was a great listener but wasn't afraid to offer his opinion or ask questions that Eddie hadn't thought about, although most of his questions did revolve around food in some way or another.

Oh, yes. Now, this is important. To the casual observer Dog's accent made him sound like most dogs, with the iconic bark, moan, or whine. However, over the years Eddie had developed the ability to understand Dog clearly, despite the heavy canine accent. Such abilities often develop between friends who spend a lot of time together. So much so, that really close friends have been known to communicate whole sentences of feelings and intentions with only a look. Such was the relationship between Dog and Eddie. So, when Dog whined in response to Eddie's comment about what Kevin had said earlier that day, it made complete sense that Eddie responded by saying...

"I don't know, maybe."

The main problem here is that I, myself,

have never had the ability to understand Dog's accent; it's simply too strong. Therefore, I cannot offer an accurate translation. All I can do is divulge the sound and inflection of Dog's barks, moans and, whines, and by doing so, give a general idea of the meaning. Anyway, Eddie continued by saying,

"But one thing's for sure, Dog, it just keeps getting weirder and weirder out there."

Dog barked in response to Eddie, which probably meant something along the lines of a "Yep" or "No kidding" or maybe even, "You can say that again." At any rate, Dog seemed to agree with Eddie's statement. And happy that Dog agreed, Eddie closed the lid to the jar, placed it back on the shelf with other like collections, and turned on his radio. The radio gave a short crackle, followed by the introduction to one of Eddie's main devotions, "Mann's Conspiracies."

8

MANN'S CONSPIRACIES

Mann's Conspiracies was a radio show hosted by Tony Mann, a legend in the world of conspiracy theories. Eddie would often use information gleaned from Tony Mann's show to help him understand the world around him, especially those things shrouded in mystery. This was important to Eddie because he felt that there were parts of his own life that were more mysterious than not.

That being said, the mysteries of commonly-held conspiracy theories had become somewhat of an obsession of

Eddie's. So much so that the walls in Eddie's room were covered in newspaper clippings, maps, articles and other researched material used to make sense of "that" key mysterious event in Eddie's past. But that story is for another time. *This* story is about Eddie and The Lizard Man, so we'll get back to that.

The theme song for Tony Mann's Conspiracies concluded as Eddie sprayed Easy Cheese on a beef stick. To his dismay, the can sputtered out the last little bit of cheese. In a frustrated motion, Eddie tossed the empty can into the trash. However, the frustration quickly subsided as he took a satisfied bite of the delicacy he called "cheese on a log" and sat back to enjoy his favorite show.

As the music faded, Tony Mann's voice bombed through the radio speaker.

"And we're back. You're listening to Mann's Conspiracies, and today we're continuing our conversation about the reptilians among us. But before we open up the lines here's a recap of a few important points."

As Tony began to list off attributes and signs of the reptilian kind, Eddie picked up a gulp-sized slush drink and took a sip.

"Number one, reptilians tend to be people with power or influence, like world leaders, CEOs, even managers of antique stores."

Eddie couldn't believe his ears.

"Kevin?" Eddie said to himself.

"That's right, your boss could be a reptilian," Tony confirmed as if speaking directly to Eddie.

Eddie's eyes grew large. He began to recall various encounters with Kevin over the years.

Tony continued with his list.

"Number two, they may have special abilities like ESP or being psychic."

Eddie's eyes grew even larger as he recollected an instance where a customer came into the store looking for a specific item.

Before the customer could finish the description of the item, Kevin said...

"'I know exactly what you're looking for.'"

And after Kevin had taken the customer to the item, the customer gasped in surprise and said...

"'Why, Kevin, you read my mind. This is

exactly what I'm looking for.'"

Eddie's mind began reeling with the possibilities.

"No way! Kevin's psychic."

Tony Mann clipped along, "Number three, they often have low blood pressure."

The hairs on Eddie's arms stood up.

"Okay, now this can't be a coincidence."

Memories of regularly picking up take-out for Kevin floated to the front of Eddie's mind. Several times he had forgotten to get extra salt packets for Kevin. This would result in a frustrated response along the lines of...

"'You forgot to get extra salt again! How many times do I have to tell you - I need it for medical reasons.'"

Just then Eddie was jolted out of his thoughts and back into the present by the loud slurping sound of his empty slush drink.

In Eddie's mind a revelation burst into being. He turned to address Dog.

"Dog, it's all making sense; Kevin's a manager, a person with influence, he can read people's minds, and he eats way too much salt for a normal person."

The revelation continued to grow as Eddie's attention went from the radio to the jar full of sheddings on the shelf just above him.

"That's it!" Eddie declared as he grabbed the jar and presented it to Dog. "These aren't snake skins, they're lizard skins! It's so obvious - the antique store doesn't have a snake problem, it has a lizard problem. Don't you see?! Kevin's a reptilian, a real live lizard man! And right here in Linemell."

Dog barked a skeptical bark. And Eddie reassured him with,

"Well, I'm like, 99.999% sure."

Dog moaned. He often played the devil's advocate. That is, unless he felt that agreeing with Eddie on a topic would result in Eddie giving him food. But in this case, Dog could see no connection between food and being agreeable, so he defaulted to being the voice of the skeptic.

Eddie knew that Dog was right. He needed more than a few circumstantial events in order to say with certainty that Kevin was a reptilian.

He slouched back in his chair and tried to think of a way that he could prove it. Then, quite directly, he remembered Kevin's phone conversation. Eddie turned back to Dog with conviction in his eyes.

"When Kevin was on the phone earlier today with that mysterious person, they made plans for something important to happen tonight at 7:00 p.m."

Just then Eddie looked down at his wristwatch. It read 6:14 p.m. He looked over at Dog.

"Kevin doesn't close shop for another fifteen minutes. If I hurry, I might be able to follow him to wherever this important thing is happening, prove he is a reptilian, and figure out why he's here."

Eddie grabbed his pen, his notebook of Particularly Interesting Findings, his camera, and rushed out the door.

Dog moaned again. It was the kind of moan a dog gives when he believes his friend is about to do something very foolish. Yes, it was with that kind of moan that Dog laid his head down on his paws and decided the best recourse was to take a nap.

9

THE BURGUNDY SUITCASES

It was now evening as Eddie slowly crept around the outside of Kennedy Antiques. He was armed with a 35mm film camera hanging around his neck and a conviction that he would finally prove his theory to be right. He headed toward the front of the store, the part that faced Main Street.

By this time the sun had set, but the parking lot was lit by street lights, so Eddie still had to do his best to stay in the shadows if he wanted to remain unseen. So far he had succeeded. As he approached the front corner of the store, he glanced down at his watch. The time read 6:30 p.m.

Eddie hoped Kevin hadn't already left the store. If he had, Eddie wasn't sure when he would get another chance to prove that Kevin was indeed reptilian. Arriving at the corner, Eddie poked his head around the edge of the brick wall where he could see the front of Kennedy Antiques. The store's interior lights had been turned out.

"Oh great, I missed him."

But then something caught his eye. The sign hanging in the door read "Open," meaning that either Kevin had forgotten to flip the sign to "Closed," or he had just turned the lights out and hadn't left yet. Eddie moved deeper into the shadows and decided to wait a few minutes to see if Kevin would emerge.

It couldn't have been more than fifteen seconds that passed when Eddie began to lose hope.

Now, you may be thinking to yourself, "Fifteen seconds? He's losing hope after only fifteen seconds?! What a lightweight!"

And if this were any other situation you would be absolutely correct. However, in the event where you find yourself spying on your boss because you believe him to be a lizard man with questionable motives, fifteen seconds can seem like an hour or maybe even an hour and a half. And that's exactly how these fifteen seconds felt to Eddie. So you see, in this situation it wasn't so strange that Eddie was beginning to lose hope. But thankfully he didn't. Because at exactly *sixteen* seconds his patience paid off.

Eddie saw something move inside the store. It was Kevin approaching the front door and flipping the "Open" sign to "Closed." He sighed with relief as his boss opened the door and stepped onto the sidewalk.

Kevin carried two large, burgundy suitcases. He set them down on the sidewalk and turned to lock the door to Kennedy Antiques. But something seemed odd to Eddie. It wasn't that Kevin set the suitcases down on the sidewalk that seemed odd. It was *how* he set them down. Anyone seeing what Eddie was seeing would have agreed.

The suitcases were handled so gingerly that one might think he was protecting something very important.

Eddie anxiously pulled the camera up to his face and snapped a few pictures of Kevin and the mysterious suitcases.

"What do you have in those creepy looking suitcases? And why are you being so careful with them?"

As those questions and others like them were bouncing around Eddie's head, Kevin picked up the suitcases and looked up and down the street to see if anyone was watching him.

Eddie ducked back behind the corner, hoping he hadn't been seen. He gave it a few seconds before taking a peek. As he did, Kevin disappeared down the alley on the other end of the building.

Not wanting to lose him, Eddie carefully pursued Kevin from a distance. After following Kevin down three alleys and two side streets Eddie realized they were now on the backside of Morgan Street about three-quarters of a mile away from the antique store.

Eddie thought to himself…

"What on earth are you up to?"

10

WET WILLIES

Morgan Street was significant because it was the street where "Cheap'n Go" was located. Cheap'n Go was significant because it was the convenience store where Eddie got his beef sticks, Easy Cheese, and slush drinks. Being so close to Cheap'n Go reminded Eddie that once he had proven Kevin was a reptilian he needed to drop by there and pick-up some more Easy Cheese.

As Eddie was making a mental shopping list of other items he needed to buy, he saw Kevin disappear down yet another alley. He cautiously approached the corner of the alley and, crouching behind a trash can, looked around the corner into a bleak, obscurely-lit passage that led to a door Kevin was nearing. It was on the backside of a large building. On either side of the door were two barred windows that had been blacked out. Stenciled on the door was a sign that read, "Authorized Personnel Only."

Eddie snapped off a couple more photos as Kevin entered the building. The door shut with a thud behind Kevin.

Eddie looked thoughtfully at the shut door. It seemed to be challenging him. Daring him. Then he let out a long, breathy sigh. The kind of sigh that someone lets out when resolving to do something truly great; like committing to train for a marathon, or asking someone to marry them, or in this case, following a suspected lizard man into a scary building. The kind of sigh that says, this might be terribly frightening, but if I don't do it, no one will. Yes, it was with that kind of sigh that Eddie mustered all of his courage and approached the door. Then with great resolve, he turned the knob and entered the building in pursuit of the truth.

~

On the other side of the door, Eddie found himself standing in what seemed to be a dimly-lit backstage area. All around him were mic stands, can lights and other such implements used for various types of stage productions. Then, he heard a voice coming from the other side of a tall black curtain that hung just a few feet in front of him. He looked around inquisitively as he was drawn to the edge of the curtain by a sudden round of laughter.

Peering around the curtain, Eddie could see a lone performer standing on a scuffed wooden stage floor lit in green, purple and blue lights. The situation started to make sense to Eddie. The person on the stage was in the middle of a stand-up comedy routine.

"Oh. I must be inside 'Wet Willies.'"

Wet Willies was a music venue and bar located on Morgan Street. It hosted an open mic night every Thursday. Eddie had never been to the place before and began to wonder what Kevin was doing there with two mysterious burgundy suitcases. This train of thought was interrupted by the same strange whirring noise he had heard earlier that day. It was coming from deeper backstage.

Eddie whispered to himself anxiously,

"Oh, no. It's already begun."

And although Eddie wasn't sure *what* had begun, he *was* sure that if lizard people were involved it wasn't going to be good. He had to find out what Kevin was up to.

"That noise, it has to be some kind of signal or communication. But what does it mean?"

For a moment fear threatened to paralyze Eddie. However, another round of laughter from the crowd on the other side of the curtain, reminded him there were people counting on him, whether they knew it or not, and backing down wasn't an option.

11

EDDIE AND THE GIANT

With renewed determination, Eddie followed the strange sound down a short hall and rounded a corner. The space was lined with more tall black curtains and was slightly wider than the corridor he just walked down. Shelves stacked with audio gear, lights, and other equipment obstructed his path, but he soldiered on.

At the end of the hall was a door cracked open. He knew that just behind it was the source of the eerie sound. Cautiously and quietly, Eddie inched across the dark room, being careful not to knock anything over.

He finally arrived at the slightly-opened door and looked in.

There was Kevin with his back to the door. He was standing over something and his arms were moving in a circular motion. The whirring tones seemed to change with each movement. And although Eddie couldn't clearly see *how* Kevin was making the noise, it was obvious he *was* making it.

"But why? What does it mean? If it is a signal, who is it for? And why Wet Willies?"

That last question sent a shiver up Eddie's spine as theory began to form.

"Wet Willies! Of course! Lot's of people gathered in one place.

The implications presented a potentially diabolical scheme.

"He's orchestrating an..."

Just then a large hand landed on his shoulder. Now, in most instances Eddie probably would have let out a loud scream due to the sheer shock of having such a large hand grab his shoulder. But this was a level of shock that exceeded all other levels of shock Eddie had ever experienced. A shock so shocking that it rendered Eddie paralyzed. He felt as if the air had been sucked right out of his lungs, leaving him breathless and therefore speechless. So speechless that even if he wanted to let out a scream, he couldn't. Then, he heard a low, gravely voice coming from behind him.

"What do you think you're doing?"

Eddie slowly turned around to see, towering over him, one of the largest human beings he had ever seen. The man was dressed in a black shirt and dark jeans. He had a scar on his face starting in the center of his left brow, running down and across his nose and ending mid-cheek. The man was terrifying. And since Eddie was still in the middle of remembering how to breathe, trying to answer the man's questions with words was proving difficult.

Eddie tried making hand motions toward the room Kevin was in. But that seemed to make the Giant Man even more upset. Then things started to get really strange as Eddie felt a slight tremor in the floor. The lights hanging from the ceiling began to sway. But the Giant Man didn't seem to notice or care, leaving Eddie to think,

"Oh my gosh, he must be in on it. I bet he and Kevin are working together. Kevin is the mastermind and this Giant Thing is the henchman. Kevin is in charge of contacting his reptilian comrades and the Giant is in charge of rounding everyone up. That's it - I've got to warn them - no matter what it takes."

Then, from the same courageous place that caused Eddie to venture down the dark hallway to Kevin's office, and with the same resolve that he had when he sighed in the alley outside Wet Willies, yes, from that place and with that resolve Eddie leapt past the Giant Man with every intention of becoming the liberator of the patrons of Wet Willies.

12

THE MOTHER SHIP

"The best laid plans of mice and men often go astray" is a popular quote about intention. The interesting thing about *intention* is that sometimes it isn't enough to accomplish the task at hand. And unfortunately for Eddie, that was the case in this situation. Because with very little effort, the Giant Man simply shifted his weight, grabbed Eddie by the collar, and pinned him against the wall as if holding a feather.

"I said, what do you think you're doing?" The giant expressed gruffly, "Were you spying on Waterboy?"

Now, being pinned against a wall, as you might expect, is an unpleasant experience for most people. However, in this case, it sent a shot of adrenaline coursing through Eddie's veins. And despite the terrifying circumstance of being in what felt like an earthquake while being threatened by an enormous - *thing*, Eddie discovered that not only had he remembered how to breathe, but he had remembered how to speak. So, with a renewed bravery and confidence, this is what he chose to say:

"You may call it spying, but I call it finding the truth! And it doesn't matter what you do to me or the other people in the building or in this town or in this world, eventually the truth will prevail!"

Of all of the explanations the Giant Man could have expected to hear come from Eddie's mouth, I can almost guarantee you *that* explanation was far beyond his wildest expectations. Which explains why the Giant Man responded to Eddie by saying...

"Are you drunk?"

In that moment, Eddie felt the atmosphere change slightly from being one of intensity to being one of possible misunderstanding. And although the room was still shaking violently and the lights were still flickering erratically, Eddie decided that maybe this Giant Man wasn't working for Kevin after all. Maybe, he was in need of saving just as much as the people on the other side of the curtain. With that new idea beginning to bloom in his mind, Eddie responded to the Giant Man's question in the following way:

"What? No! You think I'm, no I'm not..."

Before Eddie could finish, the Giant Man began ushering Eddie back down the corridor toward the exit.

"All right, let's go, kid. I think you need some fresh air."

"No, wait. Listen to me!"

Then Eddie shirked off the Giant Man and pointed across the room in Kevin's direction.

"The man in that room is a reptilian spy. If we don't stop him he's going to abduct everyone in this building so they can do tests on them!"

The Giant Man gave a sideways smile. The kind of smile a person gives when they feel sorry for you because they are thinking, "This person's elevator doesn't go to the top floor." But Eddie continued...

"Why else do you think this whole place is shaking? I'll tell you why, it's because he's in there right now communicating with the mother ship. They could be here any moment. We have to tell everyone to get out of here before it's too late!"

Suddenly, the shaking stopped. All was quiet. Well, all was quiet except for the noise of people applauding on the other side of the curtain.

13

THE CALM AFTER THE STORM

Eddie's head was spinning as he found himself in "the calm after the storm." Now, you may be saying to yourself, "I think that's the wrong phrase. Shouldn't it be, 'the calm *before* the storm?'" I assure you, I did, in fact, mean to say, "the calm *after* the storm." Here's why. As you may know, "the calm *before* the storm" refers to those tense moments just *before* something bad happens. Whereas, the lesser-known and even lesser-used phrase, "the calm *after* the storm," refers to those tense moments just *after* something bad has happened. And that was exactly the kind of calm Eddie experienced once the earthquake had subsided.

Another important thing to note is that oftentimes when people find themselves in "the calm *before* the storm," they try to predict what damage the storm will *do*. And, as you have probably already guessed, when people find themselves in "the calm *after* the storm," they try to determine what damage the storm has *done*. So, of course, when Eddie found himself in the calm after the storm, he immediately began to assess the situation. Once he had pulled his thoughts together he addressed the Giant Man.

"The earthquake! It stopped! They left. We're still here." He let out a long sigh, "Kevin must have called the abduction off. Or maybe it was never going to be an abduction at all. Maybe he got beamed up. It was an escape plan! He knew I was onto him."

Eddie turned to go back and see if Kevin was still in the room but the Giant Man stopped him. Eddie turned to look up at the man.

"Kid, Waterboy didn't get beamed up. No one was ever in danger of being abducted. And the shaking wasn't a mother ship… It was just the evening train. It comes through this time every night."

As the Giant Man finished up his explanation of events, down on the other end of the room Eddie heard the door creak open. He turned to see Kevin standing silhouetted in the doorway.

"Hello? What's going on? Eddie? What are you doing here?"

With a confused and slightly disappointed expression on his face, Eddie looked back at the Giant Man.

"But… What about the weird noises?"

~

Moments later, standing in the wing of the stage, Eddie watched from behind the curtains as Kevin performed a whirring rendition of "Mary Had A Little Lamb" on glasses filled with water.

Things being what they were, you would think Eddie would have been pleasantly surprised and even relieved that his boss wasn't helping reptilians plan an abduction of the patrons of Wet Willies. But although Eddie was surprised, it wasn't the pleasant kind. And as much as he should have been relieved, he wasn't.

No, at that moment the only thing he could think about was the fact that all of his bravery was for naught... *and* he was out of Easy Cheese.

Kevin ended his set, the audience applauded, and Eddie went home not looking forward to going into work the following day.

14

THE MORALS

The next day Eddie walked up to Kennedy Antiques holding a gulp-sized slush drink in one hand and a small Cheap'n Go bag filled with salt packets in the other. He approached the door, took a big breath and entered the store. He was greeted by an uncharacteristically pleasant Kevin.

"Good afternoon, Eddie."

"Hey, Kevin."

Eddie crossed the store and met Kevin next to a display case of various types of jewelry that Kevin had been polishing.

He handed Kevin the slush drink and salt packets unenthusiastically.

"Ah, what's this?" Kevin said in a friendly tone.

"It's an apology. For thinking you were a reptilian spy."

Kevin looked at the cup, then took a big slurp of the slush drink.

"Apology... accepted."

Then a smile appeared on Kevin's face accompanied by a sinister glint in his eye.

"After all, no one would believe you. Do you know why?"

Eddie gulped.

"Why?"

"Because I've got the people of Linemell in the palm of my scaly hand and there's nothing you can do about it."

Eddie felt the hairs on the back of his neck stand on end.

"Did he just say 'scaly hand'? I knew it! He is a reptilian!"

Just as that thought crossed Eddie's mind, it was interrupted by a loud laugh delivered by a very amused Kevin, who held his side as he continued talking through his laughter.

"Scaly hand! Get it? Because you thought I was a... Oh, what did you call it?... Oh yes, 'reptilian spy!'"

Eddie wasn't amused by Kevin's little joke but he laughed along anyway, hoping doing so would cause Kevin to think he wasn't embarrassed by the whole ordeal. After about ten seconds or so Kevin stopped laughing and let out a long, satisfied sigh.

"Well, I'm heading back to my lizard-lair to contact the mother ship. So, don't let anyone disturb me."

Feeling quite pleased with himself, Kevin snorted and turned to leave.

Eddie gave another half-hearted, nervous chuckle and went to clock in. As Eddie was writing down his start time, Kevin called back to Eddie with a hint of charm in his voice,

"On a serious note Eddie, why don't we just pretend the whole thing never happened. What do you say?"

Eddie looked up from his task to see Kevin looking at him with a sincere expression on his face. Eddie couldn't help but reciprocate the gesture with a nod and thankful smile. Kevin smiled back and headed toward his office.

Feeling ashamed of himself for letting his imagination run away with him, and for accusing his boss of being a reptilian spy, he put a little more gusto into his dusting.

And that brings us to the most important part of this story. The moral.

What Eddie learned was people like him, who have very vivid imaginations, should be careful not to let those imaginations cause them to jump to conclusions.

However, as important as that moral is, everyone knows that a good story always has two important morals. And the second important moral to every story in "The Curious World of Eddie Billings" is this: "Things are rarely as they seem."

Because, while Eddie was busy with his work, the clock on the wall struck 1:00 pm. And unbeknownst to Eddie, Kevin's bright green human eyes transformed into bright green reptilian eyes as he stepped into the dark hallway.

"The best stories never end."

Dallas Billings

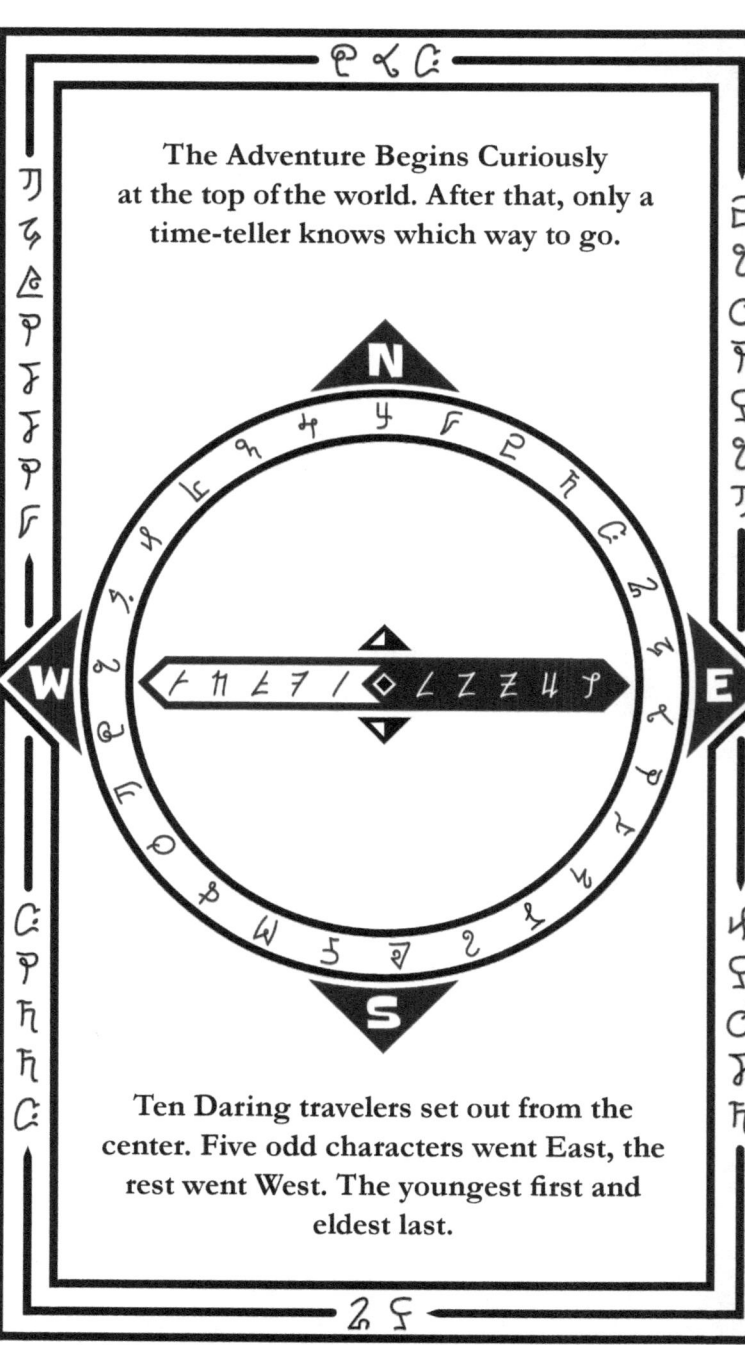

**The Adventure Begins Curiously
at the top of the world. After that, only a
time-teller knows which way to go.**

**Ten Daring travelers set out from the
center. Five odd characters went East, the
rest went West. The youngest first and
eldest last.**

Enter

The Curious World

of

Eddie Billings

visit...

linerhouse.com

ABOUT THE AUTHORS

Stefan Liner

Stefan has had a passion for storytelling his entire life. Being home-schooled from the beginning, he found the freedom to stretch his storytelling muscles often. This led him into the entertainment industry where he has acted onstage as well as on screen. He has worked on feature films, as well as written, directed and produced hundreds of commercials and music videos. He also has an award winning web-series under his belt. Quite the accomplishments for someone who struggled with reading his entire life. Eddie and the Lizard Man is the first book in a series of stories about The Curious World of Eddie Billings. Stefan lives in the beautiful mountains of Western North Carolina.

Robin Liner

Robin began her writing career as a singer-songwriter in the 1980's. But she found her way to storytelling when she began home-schooling her six children. She has published three children's books, written several feature-length screenplays (one which made the semi-finals of an international screenplay competition) and was the lead writer for an award winning web-series, When Fact Met Fiction. She has joined forces with her eldest son, Stefan, to co-write Eddie and the Lizard Man. She lives in the small town of Weaverville, North Carolina with her husband Jay and their family.